I KNOW WHAT MY CAT IS THINKING

AND IT ISN'T VERY COMPLIMENTARY

DOROTHY SEYMOUR MILLS

Barringer Publishing, Naples, Florida
www.barringerpublishing.com

ISBN: 978-0-9903935-1-1

Library of Congress Cataloging-in-Publication Data
I Know What My Cat Is Thinking / Dorothy Seymour Mills
Printed in U.S.A.

INTRODUCTION

The cat featured in this book lived with me in my New England home when I was "between husbands." I decided to bring him into my household with the notion that he might become entertaining company for me. I underwent quite an attitude adjustment when I realized that I was the one expected to provide the entertainment.

Toto—so called because my name is Dorothy—proved to be a rather intimidating companion. I soon discovered, from the expressions on his face and from his body language, that he had little respect for my efforts to become a best-selling author. Through his attitude, he showed me that he expected me to spend most of my time participating not in what I thought was my main occupation but in his, which was engaging in play. Perhaps Toto is to blame for my failure to become the Danielle Steel of New Hampshire.

Because Toto seemed to care nothing for my work, I developed the weird notion that he was my severest critic. Whenever I wrote something, I found myself re-reading it while keeping in mind the question, "What would Toto think of this?" The answer that came to me was never reassuring.

It was not until Toto left me for another old lady that I was able to pull myself together and create publishable books and articles. Even today, whenever I submit a final draft to a publisher, I sometimes think of Toto and pose that worrisome question to myself.

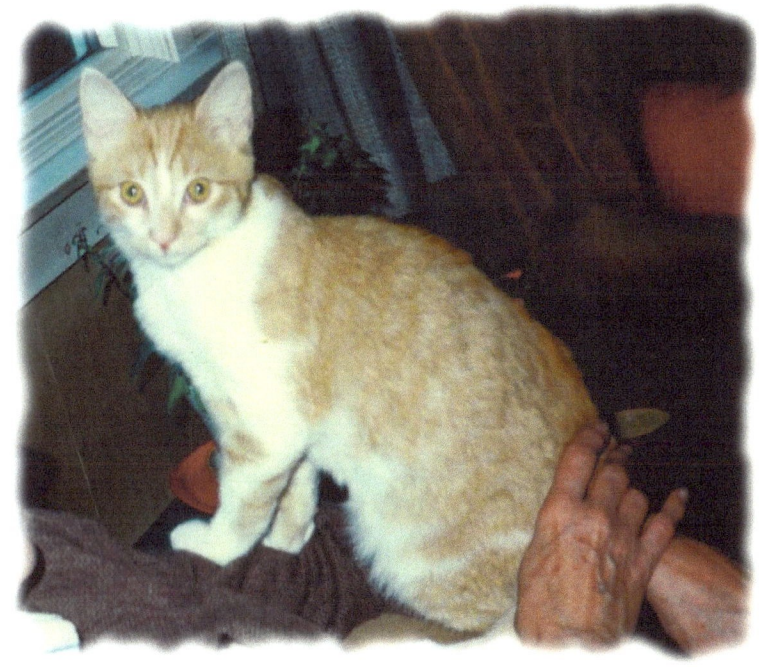

I hear a car pulling into the drive. Have you invited somebody who will disturb my cat naps?

I t's the mail carrier, probably with another rejected article.

Shall I bite the mail carrier when she opens the screen door? When are you going to give up and forget about trying to write something good? Obviously, you're not going to make it in this field.

She ran away. Scaredy-cat.

Okay, let's get at it, since you're determined to keep trying. I found my spot. You didn't like it yesterday when I reclined on that "fat" manuscript. So make some room on the crowded table for me!

Well, I don't enjoy being chased away. I'll stay up here, where I can look down at you and your manuscripts. So what are you going to do about it?

This is a better spot, too. You can go ahead with your so-called writing. I'll stay here for a while and protect my tree.

I'm tired of playing with your green editorial pencils. You can have them back now. How was I to know you needed them?

Don't tell me you're going to submit another article to those people? Will you ever give up?

They're just leading you on. This is what I think of them.

Break time! Let's play my favorite game. You can do all the seeking. See if you can find me.

Well, I don't think much of your latest effort. Did you bring it in here with you, to dispose of properly?

Can you please forget about trying to write and watch me play with my pretend mouse?

Pretty good tail, anyway. Better than your tales. Why don't you write a Tale of Two Kitties? Or even One Kitty.

Okay, so that was kind of mean. I'll hide in this brown box for a while with this foolish-looking simulated mouse, until you cool off.

Yes, that was rather vigorous play. The mouse's tail came off...so what? Relax. You're not accomplishing anything, anyway.

Did you put this cute little house here for me? I guess you forgive me for my remarks about your writing. I'm wondering if I could be an interior decorator.

You wouldn't fit in here. Go back to your table and see if you can accomplish something while I examine this. I'm thinking a light gray paint, perhaps.

With this pose for the camera, I can fool everyone into thinking I'm just an innocent little cat who never criticizes a writer's work.

Of course, I'm lying here thinking about chewing on a corner of one of your manuscripts. You don't really want them, do you?

I'm biding my time until I get back to the table and check on that article you're writing. I bet I can find something wrong with it. I'm quite good, you know.

Hey, are you about to take this beautiful new paper bag away from me? It doesn't have any of your manuscripts in it, honest.

My toy and I just fit in this bag. Go away. Get back to your table and start scribbling.

Well, have you got an idea for an article, or don't you?

If I think of a writing idea for you, will you come down on the rug and let me roll my new toy to you? I think I have some real talent.

Aw, you're no fun. Your mind isn't on the game. This empty film box is more fun!

I don't know why you keep talking to me. I'm not going to pay attention to anything you say...or write.

This painting of me that was made by your artist friend: it's okay, but I think she failed to capture the real me. She omitted any hint of my valuable critical abilities.

This is my best pose...at the kitchen window. I have decided on my career. I shall be called "The Great Critic."

ALSO BY DOROTHY SEYMOUR MILLS

The following books that Dorothy has written over the years are in print and available through her web site and from electronic sources as well as through the publishers listed below.

With Harold Seymour:
Baseball: The Early Years
(Oxford University Press, new edition 2011)

Baseball: The Golden Age
(Oxford University Press, new edition 2011)

Baseball: The People's Game
(Oxford University Press, new edition 2011)

Other work in baseball history:
A Woman's Work: Writing Baseball History with Harold Seymour
(McFarland, 2004)

Chasing Baseball: Our Obsession with Its History, Numbers, People and Places
(McFarland 2010)

Drawing Card: A Baseball Novel
(McFarland, 2012)

First in the Field: My Journey as the First Woman Baseball Historian
(Thinker Media, 2012)
e-book only

Historical novels:
The Sceptre (Patrician/Xlibris, 1998)
The Labyrinth (Patrician/Xlibris, 2003)
The Treskel (Patrician/Xlibris, 2005)

Vegetarian cookbook:
Meatless Meat: A Book of Recipes for Meat Substitutes
(Patrician/Xlibris, 2001)

Children's books:
Ann Likes Red (Purple House Press, 2001)
Ballerina Bess (Patrician/Trafford, 2002)
The Sandwich (Patrician/Trafford, 2003)